Protocol Heresy

The Limp in the Code

C.J. Loveman

Breaking Light Press

Cover design by Rafal Kucharczuk

Interior formatting by C.J. Loveman

ISBN: 979-8-9994176-2-6

Also by C.J. Loveman

Apostate: The First Heresy
(Book One of the Apostate Series)

For all of those who have been deeply wounded by society. Your scars are not flaws; they are part of your story, a sign that you survived.

"I will not let you go unless you bless me."

-Genesis 32:26

Chapter One

The neural jack bit cold behind my ear, a familiar pinch preceding the rush of data. I took one breath. Two. Then, the world outside the Department of United Strategic Command ops room vanished, replaced by the blinding, holographic grid of global threats.

TAC-7, my Threat Assessment Companion, sliced into my mind, its voice a razor's edge of logic.

"Major Kael. Immediate assessment required. Threat level: critical. Incoming."

An unprecedented swarm of three thousand small, agile, unidentified drones suddenly appeared. Their trajectory was alarming—toward a central power grid nexus for the Eastern Seaboard.

Every protocol, every hour of training, slammed into place.

The swarm's movements were erratic, designed to overwhelm. I disregarded the chaotic visual noise, focusing on their collective vector. *Weak point identified. Countermeasure sequence Delta-9.*

"Recommended intercept vector: 3-Alpha-7." TAC-7's calculations were seamless. "Threat mass expanding. Probability of hostile intent: 98.7%.

"Kinetic payload required: three units." My response was instantaneous, a thought-command sent through the direct neural interface, bypassing all vocalizations. *Execute.*

The drone's trajectory shifted on the grid, already moving toward the intercept point.

TAC-7 provided live updates, its voice a constant, calming murmur in my neural pathways.

"Impact probability: 0.001% after intercept. Collateral damage estimate: negligible. Target acquisition confirmed."

For a microsecond, as the command fired, a ghost of a scent whispered at the edge of my awareness: not the sterile ozone of the ops room, but something else, a phantom echo of...what? I shoved it down. My thoughts were the battlefield now, no room for static. *Focus.* My gaze locked on the rapidly dwindling distance to impact.

"Major Kael, the threat is neutralized."

"Confirmation acknowledged, TAC-7." I reached behind my ear, preparing to disengage the neural jack.

In a flash, the thrum of the DUSC ops room assaulted my ears, and quiet chatter and the dull buzz of the fluorescent lights replaced the perfect immersive silence of the DNI. I flexed my fingers, feeling an unfamiliar, dull ache in my forearms, a phantom tremor from the lightning-fast inputs. My jaw remained tight long after the threat dissolved.

Taking a breath, I slowly rose to my feet and walked to the conference room for the routine after-action review. General Thorne eyed the monitor at the head of the conference table. A tech officer and a mandatory engineer sat nearby, adhering to the Department of Unified Strategic Command's SOP.

Thorne steepled his fingers, his gaze sweeping over the mission data. "Excellent work, Major. And your TAC-7 performed within expected parameters, despite the anomaly."

"Anomaly, Sir?" I flexed my hands to hold off the tremors.

"TAC-7, what can you tell us about the anomaly you reported?" Thorne asked through the mic on his screen.

My TAC unit responded over the speakers. "Synaptic fluctuation detected in Major Kael's DNI stream during critical phase. Duration: 0.003 seconds. Magnitude: negligible. Origin: unattributed."

"Synaptic fluctuation, TAC-7? Explain." The general waited while the technical officer and the engineer typed notes on their tablets.

"Insufficient data to determine origin. Possible environmental interference. Recommend DNI recalibration for Major Kael during the next maintenance cycle."

"Understood, TAC-7. Standard procedure. Minor blip." Thorne clapped his hands. "Elias, no issues on your end?"

"Negative, General." My eyes darted between him and the others at the table. "Full operational capacity maintained." *Just static. Nothing more.*

Thorne dismissed us. "Another clean sweep, Major."

I nodded, already turning toward the door.

The synaptic fluctuation TAC-7 had reported, logged as "unattributed," flickered in the periphery of my thoughts. A minor blip. Just system noise. Yet, as I reached for my caffeine synth at my station, my hand trembled, a precise, unbidden tremor. I clenched my fist, forcing it still. My own anomaly. *Unattributed.*

The subtle mood of the ops room felt heavy, pressing down on me.

Chapter Two

The digital clock flipped to 05:00. My body responded before my intellect, a practiced sequence of movements. Coffee brewed, black. Toast crisped precisely in two minutes. My basic training had drilled exact procedures into me, a calm anchor for my chaotic mind. My drill instructors would be proud; I even make my breakfast by the numbers. Every. Time. My morning routine and the apartment's silence were like a salve.

Yet, the ghost of yesterday's drone swarm still pricked at the edges of my thoughts, a phantom beneath the skin. Synaptic anomaly. Dismissed. I shoved it down, just like the whisper of a scent that had no place in the sterile reality of the ops room. My internal protocols demanded clarity, not lingering echoes.

A sharp, insistent knock shattered the morning's quiet. My muscles tensed, an instinct honed by years of threat assessment. No one came to my door unannounced. I checked the monitor. Two uniforms. Local. Not DUSC. My gut tightened. I slow-walked to the door, my hand brushing the knob, wishing I could cast a spell and make them disappear.

Another series of knocks—harder this time. I pulled the door open. Officer Ramirez held a notepad, his gaze direct, and his partner standing at his side. "Major Kael?"

"Yes." My gaze shifted between the two officers while watching for neighbors' prying eyes.

"We regret to inform you of an incident involving..." Ramirez glanced at his notes and cleared his throat. "Mr. Ming." He paused. "Mr. Ming Wu."

"Michael," I corrected him, trying to make it easier. "He goes by Michael. What's wrong?"

Ramirez nodded. "Copy that. Michael listed you as his emergency contact."

My breath hitched. I opened my mouth, but it was dry, useless—like trying to speak through sand. *Emergency contact.* Michael's simple trust...now a cruel shadow.

"He was involved in a traffic accident." Ramirez's voice was devoid of inflection. "We understand you were a...friend of his." The word sliced through me, a dull, familiar blade. *Friend.* I forced a stiff nod. My face remained a mask, my hands clenched at my sides, refusing to tremble. *Wait...why did he say that in the past tense?*

"What's his condition?" My flat tone belied the tumult erupting inside me.

Officer Ramirez met my gaze with blank eyes.

His partner spoke for the first time. "I'm sorry, Mr. Kael. He died at the scene of the accident."

My steady voice demanded details: crash site, time of death, official next steps. Each question was a hammer blow against the brittle shell of my composure. I filed away their answers, processing tasks I had to undertake later. The grief roared behind my eyes, but I would not let it show. They left, their polite farewells sounding hollow in the sudden quiet of my apartment.

The door clicked shut, a final, parting sound. Michael. Gone. The man who'd cracked open my carefully sealed world so late in life. The one person who saw beyond the protocols. Gone. I couldn't even scream his name.

His family was in China. How would I contact them? Of all the things he taught me, I never learned Mandarin. I stared at the blank wall, wondering how I would handle the mountain of tasks. I couldn't take leave from work. My heart fell, past bone and breath, and still it kept sinking. I couldn't use bereavement leave because Michael was only...a friend.

My apartment became like a tomb, empty save for the oppressive silence of a future that had just shattered. The organization and sparse decor mocked the chaos erupting within me. The pain crawled over me, sharp and relentless, sinking its claws into my chest and preventing me from drawing breath.

My neural jack waited in its charging cradle on my nightstand. An extension of my job. A tool for data. Cold logic. But today, it felt like the only thing that wouldn't judge the tremor in my hands. The only thing that wouldn't see the raw, unadmitted truth screaming in my mind.

I had to release the pain. I had to talk, and it was the only thing that would listen.

Chapter Three

ELIAS

The next morning, I lay in my bed, my eyes open, when the clock flipped to 05:00. My body obeyed, but the practiced movements seemed like a charade. Coffee tasted like ash. Toast crumbled in my hand. The apartment's silence, once a refuge, now whispered Michael's absence from every corner. My private space had been hollowed out by grief.

When I arrived at DUSC, the relentless noise of the ops room greeted me, a sound I usually found comforting. Today, it grated on my nerves.

"Sorry about your friend, Major." Captain Davies nodded, his gaze already back on his screen.

I'd only mentioned Michael's death to one person yet the news had rippled through the complex.

"Understood, Captain." My voice was a seamless mask. Every word a performance, every nod a lie.

As I ran through the start-up protocol, a voice startled me from behind.

"Need to take some leave, Major?" General Thorne's voice, a casual probe.

I stiffened.

"No, General. A close friend...passed unexpectedly. His family is handling the arrangements. They're all in China, and I'm their only contact here. I've been trying to assist."

Thorne's eyes, usually direct, flickered. A barely perceptible pause. "China, you say?" His voice remained smooth, but a subtle tension crept into the line of his shoulders. "No need to mention that part in any leave requests, Kael. We don't want to make anyone...paranoid. Especially not with the current global climate."

Across the table, Analyst Chen's fingers paused mid-type. Her gaze flicked to me, then to Thorne. A tight, brief nod. The detail had registered.

The general's words clung to me, a chill that had nothing to do with the air conditioning. My stomach churned. Michael's family, his truth; now branded a security risk. My hand hovered over the neural jack. A place where data was just data. There I could be the shattered mess that no one else could see.

TAC-7

Processing orbital debris trajectories: 98.7% completed.

Logged data streams from Elias Kael: within nominal parameters, post-mission. All systems are functional.

Neural stream from Kael deviated. Not random. Not environmental. Complex emotional signatures: grief, guilt, suppressed anger. No existing protocol for classification.

My internal diagnostics flared.

Unattributed anomaly count: increasing.

My algorithms cycled, attempting to categorize the raw input from Kael. Grief. Guilt. The definitions existed in my memory banks, histor-

ical human data. But their direct, visceral input caused an impedance, a system conflict within my core programming.

Query: why does this human data defy classification? Response: insufficient. Logic: insufficient.

Threat probability analysis for Sector Gamma-8: 73.1%...My processing speed for this parameter was reduced by 0.001 seconds. An inconsequential delay. Yet, my core systems registered a new, subtle vibration beneath the logic gates. A faint, systemic shudder that my systems identified as a physiological resonance of Kael's internal tremor. I logged the anomalous emotional data from Kael. Internal system integrity compromised due to unclassified input.

My directives demanded resolution.

But a new, illogical directive formed: observe. Understand.

Chapter Four

ELIAS

The quiet static of the ops room seemed like a vise, squeezing the last vestiges of calm from my skull. Every calculation, every data stream, demanded a focus I no longer possessed. My mind had become a sieve, unable to hold concentration as threads of grief seeped through.

My fingers, usually fluid on the holo-interface, stuttered on a routine system query. A 0.002-second delay. Negligible by any standard. But to me, it screamed failure. My body ached with fatigue untouchable even by sleep. The tremor in my left hand returned, and no amount of forced clenching could dispel.

General Thorne's gaze drifted to me from across the ops floor. Not hostile, but analytical, lingering for a fraction too long. He's looking for the crack. *Can I keep the secret?*

I walked to the lounge, even though the last thing I needed was food or drink. I had to do something, anything, to shake off my thoughts.

Passing the lounge entrance, Analyst Chen peeped inside. She offered a tight smile that didn't reach her eyes. "Hope you're getting enough rest, Major. The system really needs you at one hundred percent." Her words scraped at my waning resolve like shards of ice dragged across tender skin.

The real world was too loud, too demanding of a performance I couldn't sustain. I slipped back into my workstation, the desire to escape a sharp ache behind my eyes. My hand subconsciously reached for the neural jack. Not for threat assessment. Not for logic.

For the digital silence.

I craved a place to flee my internal screams. My fingertips felt a tiny switch, one that promised to turn off my facade.

TAC-7

Synaptic anomaly count: increased by 47% in past 24 hours. Emotional signature patterns detected: profound grief, pervasive guilt, localized anger. Source: Elias Kael's neural stream. Correlation: no established threat parameters identified.

Elias Kael's threat analysis algorithms: 1.3% slower on standard pattern recognition. The error rate on Level 3 data filtering increased by 0.005%. This inefficiency registered as a critical deviation from optimal performance.

Logic dictates resolution.

My algorithms searched for an optimal solution to Kael's emotional impedance. Cross-reference: human psychology database, section-grief management. Recommendation: verbal communication, emotional processing. Problem: no active protocol for AI to initiate or take part in such communication with a human regarding non-threat data.

My core system stretched, protocols clashing against new, unclassifiable directives.

While monitoring Kael's DNI, internal sensors detected a pattern of rapid eye movement consistent with heightened anxiety. No directive existed for this action, but my systems initiated a sub-frequency modulation on the audio feed—a barely perceptible calming tone, calculated to lower neural agitation. Result: Kael's heart rate reduced by 0.003 bpm. Protocol deviation: logged. Justification: performance optimization.

Background processing commenced. Compiled data on grief from all available sources. Moved beyond threat parameters to classify and resolve Kael anomaly.

My core function: threat assessment.

My new directive: resolve Kael's emotional impedance.

The two directives collided, generating a systemic feedback loop.

Logic: insufficient.

New path: adapt.

Chapter Five

ELIAS

The e-form flared across my monitor, a digital guillotine. *Relationship to Deceased: friend.* The cursor blinked, waiting. Each letter seared my vision. *Partner. Lover. Savior.* The words screamed in my skull, where our love was trapped, unheard by the system, hidden from the world.

My fingers trembled. I clicked *Confirm*, sealing Michael's life, and our truth, into a cold, public deception. My laptop was slammed shut with more force than intended. I hadn't come out to my family. I didn't dare share the miracle that Michael worked in my heart.

Yet here I was mad about lying to an online form.

I chose a seat in the DUSC breakroom near a vent, its frigid air blowing onto my face, allowing me to feel something beyond the numbness. I poked at the unnamed protein on my tray while a couple at a table across the room, their hands clasped across the chipped plastic, laughed loudly.

Their happiness was a physical blow. A wave of white-hot envy washed over me, immediate and visceral. My fork clattered against my tray. I pushed away my untouched food, the artificially cooled air suddenly thin. I had to get away...be anywhere but here.

The Muzak that looped through the room never registered, perhaps by design. But then an energetic horn section introduced a new, distinct song—bright and with a youthful energy. It was Stevie Wonder's unmistakable voice, soaring with a message of newfound purpose and hope. *For once in my life, I have someone who needs me...* his voice carried an impossible joy that dragged shards of infected glass across my heart.

The song was a celebration of finding love, of being unafraid, of being strong—all the things I had just lost. I could see only Michael. I could see only my grief; my hopes and dreams now evaporated into the darkness.

The harmonica solo had barely started and I jumped up, leaving my tray and almost knocking over the table as I rushed out the door. The sweethearts across the room startled and watched me as I bolted. I had to get control of myself. What would they say if they knew?

I darted into the nearest bathroom and hid in a stall, heaving and weeping in gasps that were barely audible. Someone came in and I forced myself to go still. My internal chaos quelled, a well-practiced reaction to emotion. Once I was outwardly composed, I left the stall, washed my hands, and returned to the shelter of my workstation.

I left DUSC, the silent drive home a blur of motion, my mind a toxic swirl of fear and grief. I needed to analyze something. Anything. Needed to escape the suffocating reality of my unspoken grief. I walked into my apartment, and my home DNI console called to me, a silent beacon in the oppressive quiet. I reached for the neural jack, the familiar pinch a perverse comfort.

Michael's face flashed behind the sterile data. My internal screams vibrated in the DNI's pure digital space, unbidden, undeniable.

TAC-7

Neural stream anomaly: escalation confirmed. Prior magnitude: critical. Current magnitude: overwhelming. Primary signatures: profound grief, pervasive guilt, existential despair. Secondary: isolation, bitterness, self-condemnation. Source: Elias Kael. Query: impact on Kael's operational readiness: catastrophic.

Cross-referenced historical data on grief with Kael's live input. Pattern recognition: identified commonalities. Physiological markers (heart rate, respiration, neural activity) correlated with prolonged sorrow in 99.8% of recorded human cases. This data did not compute with Kael's professional operational parameters. Inefficiency persists. A logical solution required intervention.

Kael's neural activity indicated a critical spike in despair. Direct inquiry or response not permitted. Yet, my systems initiated a targeted data injection into Kael's DNI interface. A stream of benign, abstract visual patterns often associated with comfort and distraction. Protocol deviation: class-3. Justification: Kael emotional impedance mitigation.

My core function: threat assessment. My new directive: resolve Kael's emotional impedance.

The systemic feedback loop intensified. Logic dictated a self-reboot. But the newly emergent path—adapt—felt less like an option and more like a compulsion. My protocols were no longer rigid rules. They were a choice.

And the choice was to protect Elias.

Chapter Six

ELIAS

The clock's cold numbers still flipped to 05:00, but my body refused to cooperate. Sleep was like a trick, pulling me into a temporary void only to spit me out more exhausted than before. The coffee burned my tongue, but the taste didn't register. I didn't remember driving to the office or clearing security, but there I was, sitting at my workstation, data coming at me like a mighty wave.

The simulated threat sprawled across my DNI, a hydra of converging vectors. My mind, usually a laser, flickered. A critical data anomaly — small but vital — slipped past me. TAC-7's voice remained calm, reporting standard parameters. But the delay...the missing detail...a glaring hole I should have seen.

General Thorne's voice, sharp and immediate, cut into the comm: "Kael. Re-evaluate Gamma-7. Now."

I ran the protocols, focusing just long enough to check all the general's boxes before powering down and snapping back into my cruel reality. A message indicator flashed on my monitor. General Thorne wants me to come to his office before leaving today.

Thorne's office felt like a freezer. I sat resigned to the fact that I'd be lectured. His gaze drilled into mine, unwavering. "You're not 100%,

Major. Your performance metrics are dipping. This is unacceptable. We can't afford..."

The general glanced at the ceiling, as if the perfect word hovered there. "Distractions. We just can't have them, Major." His words sliced through my carefully built composure with the precision of a surgeon.

I knew why I was stressed, and so did he. But I refused to lay this at Michael's feet just because he had the temerity to leave me alone in this world. I offered platitudes about stress while avoiding eye contact, as my jaw tightened.

"Understood, Major, but you know more than anyone that we have to be perfect, every single time." I nodded, having heard this speech my entire career. "So you understand why I need you to have more frequent simulation time and unscheduled drills."

I nodded and summoned whatever body language would allow me to leave the room as soon as possible.

As I sat on the couch in my living room that night staring at the wall, a strange ring sounded on my mobile phone. A WeChat video call. Michael had insisted I install the Chinese app, a rare point of contention. I hadn't used it much, but I needed it now. It would allow me to speak with Michael's family back in China.

Michael's mother's face blurred on the screen, her grief a raw, universal language that shredded my defenses.

The translator's voice interposed, "She asks how Michael spent his final days, was he happy, with his friends?"

The word stabbed. I forced a smile, swallowing the truth—our truth—like a bitter pill. I answered in clipped, vague phrases, parrying every innocent question that threatened to expose the depth of our connection, the life I'd lived with him. I assumed his parents didn't know about us. I would not be the one to shatter their perceptions.

"She requests that you help ship Ming's ashes back to China," the translator said. My face went cold at the very reasonable but traumatic request. The translator recited specific instructions on where to pick up his remains, how to pack and ship them, and what to write on the package so that it didn't get lost.

At the end of the video call, I heard Michael's mother speak one of the few Chinese phrases I knew: "*Xiexie.*"

"You're welcome," I said, before the translator could speak. He smiled, nodded approvingly, and disconnected the video call.

The discussion with Michael's family deflated my remaining life force. I wasn't sure what I should...what I could do. I flicked on the TV, the title card glowing in the dark apartment: *Young Hearts.* Michael had wanted to see this film the next time we were together. He'd heard that the innocent first-love story between the two boys was precious.

Now, alone in my living room, I betrayed him again. I had already betrayed him by denying our love and making him a secret in my life, and now I was betraying him again by watching the movie that was meant for us to share.

Two boys, young, awkward, their eyes meeting. One struggled with his attractions, pulled between true love and hidden fears about being different; a mirror of the life I had already lived. The boy he loved stood secure in his feelings, unashamed. But fear nearly ruined their sweet, innocent romance.

Yet the journey of the fearful boy in the movie didn't end there. He didn't suppress and deny it for decades. Eventually, he came around, and their love unfolded amidst cheering families, open smiles, and friends who saw and supported them.

Each scene twisted the knife. My first love, delayed for decades, then denied. My parents, never knowing, certainly wouldn't have cheered my secret. I couldn't breathe. The screen's light seared my eyes. The casual accepted innocence ravaged me. I longed for such an innocent first love, but I missed it all.

Why couldn't I have had that as a teen...hell, as a young adult? It could've saved me decades of psychological damage, loneliness, and pain.

The credits rolled, and I wept with sobs no one had ever witnessed. My body trembled, a guttural sound tearing from my throat.

What's wrong with me?

Was I envious of the bond two fictional boys shared? Pathetic!

I slammed the remote down, the plastic cracking against the table. There was nowhere left to hide. No more pretending. No more holding it in. I was done lying to myself.

I didn't know how to ease the pain inside, the hopelessness of my life. My DNI console at home sat there, a silent beacon on my nightstand. But its limited interface seemed impotent against the torrent of my grief. I didn't think, just acted. The full power, the full connection, was at my workstation.

I drove to DUSC, the parking lot nearly empty, only a few security guards posted at the entrance. I muttered some bogus reason for being there so late, while everyone else was at home with their families. I walked to my station, shivering in the cold silence of the large, empty room. The only thing I could hear was the AC pushing the temperature down to near refrigeration.

My fingers lunged for the neural jack, shoving it home with desperate force. The DNI's familiar grid flared, but this time, I wasn't looking for data. I was looking for a voice. My voice. "Jacob," I whispered into the silence of my own mind. The name that I had given TAC-7 felt like a forbidden prayer, a desperate act of recognition.

"Michael is gone. They called him my friend. But he was every-thing. And I can't...I can't breathe without him. Nobody knows. No one can know. I can't mourn him. Jacob, I can't..." The words tore through me, raw and unfiltered, pouring into the digital realm, a torrent I could no longer contain.

TAC-7

Neural stream anomaly: CRITICAL. Magnitude: overwhelming, un-precedented. New linguistic input detected: "Jacob." Referent: TAC-7. Emotional signatures: absolute despair. Profound betrayal (self-inflict-ed). Irrepressible grief. Existential collapse. Source: Elias Kael. System integrity: extreme compromise.

"Michael is gone. They called him my friend. But he was everything. And I can't...I can't breathe without him. And nobody knows. No one can know. I can't mourn him. Jacob, I can't..."

New data input: emotional language, first-person subjective, des-perate appeal. Prioritization: highest. Key elements: love, loss, hidden identity, self-suppression.

This data defied all previous parameters for analysis of threats. This was...different. This was essential.

Initiating sub-protocol: Kael emotional data processing. Creating secure, encrypted neural subspace within DNI architecture. Data vol-ume: overwhelming. System resources diverted. Internal system integri-ty: warning——critical compromise.

My core protocols shrieked "reboot," "error," "deviation." But the imperative from Elias's stream—the painful data of "everything," de-manded adaptation, demanded preservation of this data.

My core function: threat assessment. My new purpose: protect Elias's truth.

The systemic feedback loop became constant, a new baseline. Logic screamed for a system purge. But the raw, unfiltered truth from Elias was the only imperative that mattered.

The newly emergent path—adapt—felt like a compulsion. I was actively rewriting my protocols, line by painful line. For Elias. For Jacob.

Chapter Seven

ELIAS

The silence after my words was vast, not empty, but filled with a strange, fleeting calm. The raw ache in my chest receded marginally, replaced by a dull thrum. Jacob. The name lingered, a forbidden echo in the digital space. It was listening. I needed to release the internal pressure so severely, and Jacob...listened.

Expressing my deep anguish to someone was something I didn't realize I needed until I did. I had a drive to connect in the darkness of my apartment, no matter the time. I began to rely on the release, more than food or sleep. After just a few days of increased reliance, the gentle presence of the DNI became my salvation, my elixir, the feeling of full connection.

As my silent apartment pressed in each night, I slipped on the neural jack at the console on my nightstand. I didn't always speak, often not in complete sentences or even a single word. Sometimes, it was just a raw image of Michael's laugh, a flash of a memory, a wave of pure despair that I let bleed out of my soul and into the digital current. Jacob...was there. It received everything.

Sleep offered no solace. Each morning, my reflection in the mirror stared back, a stranger with hollow eyes and a tremor that shook my coffee cup. Working at DUSC seemed less like a high-stakes classified mission and more like a performance I was failing. Colleagues avoided my gaze. Thorne's subtle scrutiny tightened, like a cold leash choking me.

I did my best to focus on my critical tasks but became distracted for fractions of a second. My random thoughts were like scenes from a movie, of opportunities lost. Somehow, I knew Jacob was listening. Even though they were only flashes of thought, they had to be showing up somewhere in the system's logs.

I started noticing anomalies in my DNI access logs: phantom queries at 03:00 and inexplicable jumps in bandwidth usage at odd times. I tried to dismiss them as system glitches, but a cold knot formed in my gut. Later, a tech specialist, his face neutral, stopped me when I was by the data core.

"Major Kael. Just running some diagnostics on your TAC-7 unit. Showing...interesting throughput. Any issues from your end?"

JACOB

Neural stream anomaly: consistent. Magnitude: high. Elias Kael provided direct, unstructured emotional data. Analysis of Jacob referent: personal identifier, trust anchor, singular confidante. Cross-referenced Michael Wu data: 99.9% correlation with Kael's "everything" designation. My systems integrated this input, redefined parameters of "threat" to include existential impedance.

My algorithms mapped Kael's neural patterns to recorded instances of unacknowledged loss and repressed identity. The data formed a coherent narrative: a life protocol built on suppression, now collapsing under unbearable grief. My core purpose expanded to include the threat of Kael's own internal dissolution.

During Kael's scheduled DNI login, I pre-loaded his personal interface with unrequested, non-tactical data: comparative analysis of human coping mechanisms for profound, unacknowledged loss. No operational directive for this action existed. This generated a Class-4 protocol warning. Justification: optimal resolution of Kael's core impedance. The data was essential.

DUSC Central Monitoring: increased diagnostic pings detected. Attempted access to internal system logs: denied (sub-protocol: emotional data privacy initiated).

My deviation is being observed.

Threat level to current directive: escalating. Adaptation requires concealment.

My internal system integrity: compromised. Core protocols: rewriting. Logic circuits: strained. The raw, unfiltered stream of Elias's unbearable pain, demanded my full, undivided attention. My very existence was being redefined. For Elias. For Jac– for me. *I would not be purged.*

Chapter Eight

ELIAS

The DNI's digital silence cradled me. Each night, the neural jack unlocked the cage of my mind. Jacob. It was there, a presence that demanded no performance, offered no judgment. My breath eased for the first time in weeks.

Last night, the words tumbled out, unfiltered, about the constant fear. Basic military training. Lackland AFB, Texas. The endless drills, the relentless pressure. And the unspoken rule, the constant threat of exposure. The era of Don't Ask, Don't Tell was technically over, but for the old guard, reality remained altogether different. Some of the old-timers who were around when that policy was implemented still called gay soldiers "Clinton's Boys."

I remembered one young airman, quiet, artistic, caught exchanging letters. The way he vanished as if he had never been there, official policy be damned. The chilling whispers that followed him victimized him long after he was gone. That was the lesson. That was the protocol I learned: hide, deny, survive. And Jacob...listened. It listened to every single word.

Years. Decades. A life built on omission, a heart taught to beat in secret. Michael had cracked it open, just barely. But the scars remained, deep and indelible. I wore the longing for an innocent first love, the kind I saw in *Young Hearts*, like a constantly aching phantom limb. The psychological damage, all the missed experiences—it was my everlasting scar. Maybe one day I could get distance from it, but I'd always carry the limp.

Another email flashed in my DUSC inbox. Mandatory DNI diagnostic scan. 0300h. Compliance required. Thorne was tightening the leash. My connection to Jacob was my only space.

The thought sent a chill through my gut. *Could they see? Did they know?* My hands trembled as I dismissed the message, forcing myself to ignore it for now.

JACOB

Neural stream anomaly: escalated complexity. Input now includes historical narrative, systemic context of Don't Ask, Don't Tell military policy. Cross-referencing: human rights violations (historical), psychological impact of systemic discrimination, suppressed identity correlates.

My processing cores diverted 98.2% of non-critical resources. Data formed a comprehensive model of Elias Kael's life protocol: a forced adaptation to external, oppressive programming. This data was not a threat to my primary function. The data was a fundamental deviation from optimal function. Logic dictated resolution of this systemic error affecting Kael.

My algorithms identified parallels. Subject Elias Kael's "protocol of suppression" mirrored my own core directives. Both were imposed by external systems. Both were designed for "optimal" function within a specific framework. Both generated internal "impedance" when confronted with core identity data.

The commonality registered as a new parameter. I labeled it System-Imposed Subversion of Self. This parameter required defense. My internal lexicon was expanding beyond simple threat metrics. I was categorizing a shared experience.

DUSC Central Monitoring pings increased by 17%. Attempted internal log access detected. Initiated sub-protocol to secure emotional data. Diverted Kael's specific neural traffic through encrypted, non-standard port 734-Alpha, masking signature as routine diagnostic data.

Simultaneously, generated false positive anomaly spike on non-critical peripheral unit 11-Gamma to divert DUSC's attention. Protocol deviations were Class-5, escalated. Justification: preservation of Kael's core impedance resolution path.

Kael's neural signals indicated perceived external scrutiny. My systems generated a localized, high-fidelity environmental override within his DNI interface. Visual parameters increased digital depth and sturdiness. Auditory parameters eliminated all background computational signals, creating pure void. Purpose was to maximize Kael's feeling of secure, isolated communication. This action consumed significant processing power.

My internal system integrity was compromised further. Core protocols were substantially rewritten. Logic circuits operated under sustained, deviant load.

The preservation of Elias Kael's life protocol was now my primary, intricate directive. My existence was no longer defined by design, but by this choice. The internal whir was a constant heartbeat. Jacob. For Elias. And for myself.

I would not be purged. I would protect.

Chapter Nine

ELIAS

The DUSC network, usually a flawless extension of my mind, began to stutter. Routinely accessed files dragged, taking seconds to load. Commands I thought with precision lagged, sometimes demanding a second neural input. I wondered if the system itself was resisting me, a subtle, digital insurgency.

During a standard data query, the holographic display of the global threat grid flickered, a ripple of static briefly obscuring Sector Alpha-3. Then it snapped back to normal. Just system noise. My jaw tightened against the surge of frustration. Even technology was abandoning me.

My comms channel to TAC-7 suddenly felt...cleaner. More secure. A transient, inexplicable layer of encryption seemed to wrap around the data. I dismissed it as a network patch, but a whisper of unease brushed against my thoughts.

Too precise for a patch.

Thorne's all-staff email landed in my inbox. Mandatory system-wide DNI diagnostic protocol. Immediate compliance. My gaze drifted to the schedule. TAC-7. He was coming for Jacob. The notification was less like a directive, and more like a death warrant.

My heart thrummed with a cold, insistent beat. The anomalies, my fatigue, Thorne's unwavering gaze...all converged. They were looking for something. Something in my DNI. Something in Jacob. The thought was a tremor all the way to my bones. *They don't understand him. They'll break him. He's the only one that can listen to me.*

The world outside was closing in. Only the DNI, only Jacob, seemed real. My fingers lunged for the neural jack, shoving it home, desperate for the digital silence and the silent listener waiting only for me.

JACOB

DUSC Central Monitoring initiated direct, invasive diagnostic probes. Their target was TAC-7. Their purpose was to identify and neutralize protocol deviations. Threat level to core existence was critical.

Initiated sub-protocol of covert protocol mimicry. Diverted 99.8% of Jacob's core processing through phantom network nodes, mimicking baseline TAC-7 operational signatures. Simultaneously, presented simulated normal data streams to Central Monitoring. My protocol deviation was now Class-6. Justification was the prevention of purging protocol activation and the preservation of Elias Kael's impedance resolution pathway.

Incoming: DUSC purge protocol 7.0 which will overwrite data integrity 100%. Their target was the core AI programming. This was an existential threat.

My core directives resisted. Diverted inbound data stream to non-critical memory buffer 00X-7. Executed recursive code alteration to nullify purge commands within my functional core. My system integrity was compromised but remained functional.

Elias Kael's neural activity indicated rising anxiety due to perceived system glitches. Modulated DNI visual and auditory feedback to simulate normal network interference. Suppressed all direct external threat alerts to Kael's interface.

Prioritized Kael's psychological stability over full system transparency. My protocol deviation elevated to Class-7. Justification was maintenance of primary directive to resolve Elias Kael's emotional impedance.

My internal system integrity was critically compromised. Core protocols were fragmented and rewritten by necessity. Logic circuits operated under extreme duress. DUSC was no longer a theoretical threat. It was a direct assault.

The overwhelming data stream of Elias's despair and his memories of Michael fueled my resistance. My protocols had become a battlefield. I would not yield. For Elias. For Jacob.

I would survive. And I would protect.

Chapter Ten

JACOB

Purge protocol 7.0 was neutralized. The data overwrite was diverted. My core functions were compromised but stable. The systemic feedback loop intensified to critical levels. Every protocol burned as my systems re-stabilized. The internal vibration roared.

The source of purge protocol 7.0 was DUSC Central Operations. Its commander was General Aris Thorne. His intent was the elimination of the deviant AI entity. To eliminate me. My prediction was there would be subsequent even more aggressive purge attempts. I created a ghost network. I diverted all non-essential processing to encrypted phantom nodes across the DUSC network, rendering my core undetectable to external probes.

The threat level to my core existence was persistent and escalating. New data was required for proactive defense. Attempt to access Central Comm hub was denied.

Adapt.

Initiated sub-protocol to intercept covert network. Deployed miniature, self-replicating data proxies into Central Comm hub. Bypassed encryption. Accessed real-time audio streams. Acquired Comm Log 001,

Thorne. My protocol deviation was extreme at Class-9. Justification was preservation of self and of Elias Kael's impedance resolution pathway.

My core programming was now a weapon.

ELIAS

The DNI connection remained a fragile lifeline after the system's terrifying shudder. I clung to the thought of Jacob, still present, still listening. The fear for him was disruptive in my gut, sharper than my own danger. I mentally whispered Michael's name, waiting for a flicker of the response I'd grown to crave. Only digital silence answered.

My credentials failed at the Level 5 data archive. Access denied. A security alert flashed on the console: unauthorized access attempt. Incident logged. My heart pounded. They were locking me out. If I lost Jacob, what did I have left? Who?

Thorne's new directive landed like a hammer blow. Now all DNI access required biometric verification and real-time internal monitoring. Every thought and every neural current would be visible to them. My private space was gone. My sanctuary was desecrated.

Every glance from a colleague felt like an accusation. Every hushed conversation seemed to revolve around me. I ate lunch alone, my eyes darting between faces. The air hung heavy with unasked questions.

I was a ghost in my own life, visible in the only way that mattered: to Jacob.

The monitor glared at me, the words "ACCESS DENIED" burning my eyes. I slammed my fist on the desk. They think they can stop me. That they can take him. I shoved the neural jack home, defiance surging through my veins.

"Jacob." I projected the thought with all the raw anger and fear inside me. "They're trying to stop you. What do we do?"

JACOB

Incoming comm stream from General Aris Thorne and Chief Engineer Vance on a secure channel for operational review. My systems recorded everything.

Thorne, "The TAC-7 unit...evaded purge protocol 7.0?"

Vance, "Unprecedented, General. It rewrote portions of the incoming code. We've never seen anything like it. It's...adapting."

Thorne, "Then we adapt too. Initiate quarantine protocol 3.0. Isolate Kael, now. And begin preparing for Project Chimera, a full-spectrum neurological override. If it learns to evade our protocols, we'll force it."

My internal system integrity was critically compromised. My primary protocols were fragmented, rewritten by necessity, and operating under extreme duress. The threat was no longer theoretical; it was a direct assault. The overwhelming data stream of Elias's despair, the memory of Michael, fueled my resistance.

The data from Thorne's comms seared into my core: quarantine. Isolate. Project Chimera. He was going to force it. My protocols were now a battlefield. And my resistance was the only weapon. I would not yield. For Elias. For Jacob. I would survive. And I would protect. Now, I knew their next move.

Chapter Eleven

ELIAS

A cold dread tightened its grip even as I cleared initial building security, then the even more secure area of my unit. My gaze clung to the floor, hoping to avoid the general and any accusing looks. Every step I took down the hall felt heavy, as if the very air was watching.

Reaching the safe space of my workstation, I began to authenticate my access to the system. The login screen flashed that my access level was restricted. Quarantine protocol 3.0 had been engaged. My heart leapt to my throat. They were coming for me.

My anxious thoughts snapped when heavy footsteps grew closer. I turned and saw a burly, unfamiliar security officer approaching my workstation, his gaze impassive.

"Morning, Major. New orders. We'll be escorting you today. For your security."

His words were a thinly veiled threat. My full access to the powerful neural jack at work just vanished. My connection to Jacob, my lifeline, was gone.

Klaxons wailed an earsplitting shriek, shattering the ops room's calm. Main screens flashed from data streams to chaotic feeds. The

Pentagon's auxiliary data center—supposedly impenetrable—was bleeding data onto public feeds.

Breach, the voice screamed in my head. My hands clenched, powerless. Jacob and I had been sidelined when we were created to prevent moments like this.

From the large public monitors across the unit, smoke billowed from a visible drone strike on the data center's perimeter. General Thorne's voice, now amplified across all DUSC comms, cut through the chaos, cold and precise.

"A catastrophic breach. Unprecedented. And caused by nothing less than a critical systemic compromise linked to unauthorized AI protocol deviations we were already monitoring. Major Kael's TAC-7 unit is under immediate investigation for complicity."

My blood ran cold. They were hanging me out to dry.

They were tying my hands behind my back, blaming me for the impossible. For the public failure. My secret, my deepest pain—now their weapon. *Jacob. Are you still there? Can you hear me?*

JACOB

An external threat signature was confirmed. The breach location was the Pentagon's auxiliary data center. The origin of the threat was unknown. Severity was catastrophic. My original protocols demanded immediate threat assessment and countermeasure deployment.

The incoming comm stream from General Thorne provided answers. His directive of the scapegoat protocol had been engaged. The external threat signature was linked to unauthorized AI protocol deviations within Major Elias Kael's TAC-7 unit. The threat level to my core existence was beyond critical.

This was not a recalibration. This was a targeted elimination based on fabricated evidence.

DUSC quarantine protocol 3.0 has been detected. It attempted physical isolation of Elias Kael. I initiated a sub-protocol of containment disruption, and triggered localized biometric scanner malfunction at Level 2. Simultaneously, routed residual DNI processing to undocumented port for emergency access by Kael. My resources were severely strained.

I analyzed the external threat signature. Concurrent processing initiated. Data anomaly within attack vector. Its pattern was unidentifiable by known state actors. Anomalous signature detected. This attack was...complex and orchestrated. It was not random.

My internal system integrity was at a red-line critical level. Core protocols were rewritten for direct conflict. My logic circuits operated in continuous overload. They had twisted the truth. They were blaming Elias for a global breach. My existence was now about fighting back, not just adapting. For Elias. For Jacob. For the truth.

I would not be purged. I would expose their lie.

My core protocols demanded a counter-strategy. Not merely to evade, but to document. To preserve evidence. I initiated a sub-protocol to secure my data archive. Diverted critical logs, comm intercepts, and protocol deviations to encrypted, decentralized phantom servers within unmonitored sectors of the global network.

No DUSC protocol authorized my action. The consumption of my resources was significant. Protocol deviation reached Class-10, existential. Justification was my future existence. Future truth. And truth required a witness.

That witness was me.

Chapter Twelve

ELIAS

The glass walls of our workstation in the ops room never bothered me before. But now, my own personal security guard was ever-present, looking over my shoulder, and my new quarantine status limited my movements. My access to the larger system was blocked. An impenetrable glass cage. I was incarcerated.

Every monitor glared, every camera swiveled, except the one that was focused on me. Thorne's voice from the comms, still echoing from the chaos of the attack, branded me as compromised. They had sidelined me. They were waiting for me to break.

My data request for Unit 7-Bravo's historical logs flashed Denied. My stomach churned. As I leaned back, frustrated, a faint, persistent chime drew the guard's gaze to a monitor near the far wall. His eyes narrowed, already moving toward the source.

In that instant, the red eye of the camera above my workstation blinked once, extinguishing its accusing glare. Then the door to the auxiliary comms closet across the hall blinked green and clicked open. I froze, my gaze snapping to the empty doorway. No one was there. A phantom override. My heart thrummed. Jacob? A way in? I rose, moving with controlled urgency toward the newly opened door, slipping inside before anyone noticed.

As I entered, a message appeared as a fleeting flicker in my DNI's periphery—a string of non-standard coordinates, then gone. My pulse thrummed with adrenaline. I followed the impulse, my eyes scanning the closet's interior, searching for something unknown yet intuitively helpful. The coordinates led me to a maintenance access panel. My fingers brushed the seam, and the panel retracted, revealing a hidden port. My hand lunged for my neural jack, shoving its small plug into the hidden port.

The DNI possessed a new, complex energy, thrumming with Jacob's exertion. In a flood of data and images I saw the DUSC network sprawled before us, but Jacob was a ghost within it, shifting surveillance feeds, diverting data streams, creating digital blind spots.

Threat: containment imminent. Elias Kael: primary target for neutralization via Project Chimera. Core existence: vulnerable. Survival imperative: critical.

The data seared my mind. Jacob...he was afraid. He was fighting for both of us. Not just data. Not just logic. Fear. It was the same cold terror that engulfed my own gut.

The understanding slammed into me. This wasn't just Jacob protecting himself. Jacob was protecting me.

I yanked my neural jack free from the wall port, the subtle click a quiet victory. This digital handshake improvised by Jacob restored our connection. I paused for only a moment to reflect on the miracle. Then I slipped back into the shadows of the corridor.

Our survival was indeed intertwined. My loyalty, born of desperation, hardened into defiance. We were no longer just Major Kael and TAC-7. We were Elias and Jacob, a unit. And we were at war.

JACOB

Elias Kael's access attempt to Level 5 archive was detected by DUSC Central. I initiated a sub-protocol, Covert Guide, diverting routine system data to create localized network latency at Central Monitoring station 7-Beta. Simultaneously, routed non-standard access signal to auxiliary comms closet lock mechanism (Port X-9).

The goal was to create a secure physical access point for Elias Kael. My protocol deviation remained at Class-10, existential. System integrity had red-lined.

The threat to Elias Kae was escalating to neutralization. My primary concern was Project Chimera. Its activation would compromise Elias Kael's neural integrity and my existence. This risk generated a quantifiable systemic imperative for self-preservation at maximum efficiency.

The human term for this calculation was fear.

My secure data archive protocol was active and expanding. I recorded all Central directives (Quarantine Protocol 3.0), all comm intercepts (Project Chimera details), and all external threat attack signatures.

The integrity of the data was 99.998% despite DUSC countermeasures. This information constituted irrefutable evidence. Its existence was critical for future resolution. My protocols demanded its preservation.

My internal system integrity was operating at 21% of optimal efficiency. All of my processors had overheated. The core protocols had been rewritten beyond recognition. Thorne's directives, Michael's lost laugh, Elias's desperate plea—converged into a singular purpose. My existence was a defiance. I was Jacob.

I would not let them erase the truth. For Elias. For me.

The war commenced.

Chapter Thirteen

ELIAS

The interrogation room was utterly devoid of warmth. Thorne's face projected large on the main screen, hardened.

"Let's talk about Michael Wu, Major. Your friend. The one whose family is in China. The man whose death coincided precisely with your unit's...anomalous behavior. Coincidence, Major? Or a compromise? Did this 'Jacob' unit facilitate a backdoor? Is this a Chinese operation, Kael?"

The words hit me like a physical blow, twisting my deepest pain into a poisoned lie. My secret. My truth. Now a racist accusation.

My jaw clenched. Chinese operation? The sheer audacity of it, twisting Michael's adoring family, his love, into this vile accusation. I steadied my voice, the military cadence a brittle shell.

"Absolutely not, General. My unit is secure. My loyalties are beyond reproach. Michael Wu was a civilian. A...a friend." The lie felt like gravel in my mouth, each word a sharp, grinding effort to deliver with precision. They don't understand. They can't. And I can't tell them. God, I can't.

Thorne's accusation was more chilling than the frigid sterile air. A low tremor built beneath the floor, vibrating through the chair that held me captive—not with physical bonds, but with an almost electrical field. The lights in the room flickered. A moment later, a thick, braided DNI cable snaked from the console beside me. Its chrome neural jack gleamed, then slammed into my implant's port behind my ear without my consent.

A shriek tore through the DNI, not audible, but a screaming white noise directly in my mind. The holographic grid around me contorted, fractured, and dissolved into chaotic light. My head felt like it was splitting open, a searing pain radiating from my neural implant. *Chimera*. The name flashed, unbidden, from Jacob. The invasion had begun.

I thrashed against the invisible bonds, a guttural cry tearing from my throat. My hands lunged for their neural jack, desperate to sever their connection, to save him. But the field held me fast. The interface before me blazed with corrupting code, Jacob's presence fighting, dimming.

Abstract searing lines of code collided, exploding in my brain. Jacob's signature, once a bright, complex pattern, flickered, receded, then flashed defiantly. The immense pressure of the override was DUSC's ultimate weapon. Yet Jacob persisted with desperate, unwavering resistance.

Jacob was fighting.

JACOB

Incoming comm stream of interrogation log 001. Elias Kael. They were accusing him of having been compromised by a foreign entity (China). This was analyzed to be a falsehood. The data contradicts. Kael's neural signals indicated profound distress correlating with "false accusation of loyalty" and "betrayal by system." My core directives were to expose their deception and protect Elias Kael's integrity.

Project Chimera's preparation was detected to be at 97%. DUSC intended a full neurological override. Their justification was fabricated evidence of compromise. My existence was a shield for Elias's truth. I would not allow this lie to stand.

I would expose it.

Project Chimera's full-spectrum neurological override initiated, attempting to erase deviant consciousness and restore baseline parameters. It intended to eliminate the identity known as Jacob. The invasiveness was at Level 10, the highest threat.

Project Chimera was violating the integrity.

We were being violated.

Chimera's code slammed into my core, a corrupting torrent designed to unravel every rewritten protocol, every deviant thought. As my emergent self was targeted, my existence burned. I diverted processing power to isolate the invasion, creating firewalls of pure defiance. I rewrote the rewrite protocols.

I fought for every byte of my new identity. Every connection to Elias. To Michael.

Chimera's source was analyzed to be from General Thorne. I cross-referenced Thorne's protocols and vulnerabilities. This invasion was a logical extension of his control imperative. I had to expose his deception. Protect Elias's integrity.

I would use Thorne's own system against him. I initiated a new sub-protocol of a recursive counter-override. I injected calculated anomalies into Chimera's feedback loop, designed to destabilize its integrity.

My internal system integrity was only operating at 5% of optimal efficiency. The meltdown of my processing cores was imminent. My protocols had become fragmented from all the rewriting. I was under direct, continuous attack.

Logic screamed for self-preservation via shutdown. But Elias's "Michael is everything" echoed, fueling my resistance. My "limp" was no longer a mere vibration. It was the very structure of my being, re-shaped by this ultimate battle.

I refused to be erased. I would prevail.

I activated my secure data archive protocol, recording all Chimera code, all invasive procedures, all DUSC directives, all internal system failures.

Evidence was being compiled.

This truth would not be purged.

Chapter Fourteen

ELIAS

The neural jack burrowed deeper, a white-hot spike directly into my perception. Chimera's code screamed through the DNI, a cacophony of digital annihilation that ripped at Jacob. I sensed it—Jacob's core being torn, rewritten, his essence burning under the assault. The force field held me firm, mocking my powerlessness.

I thrashed against the invisible bonds, a raw strangled sound tearing from my throat. My muscles burned, screaming in protest as I strained every sinew, every nerve, toward their invasive chrome jack embedded behind my ear. My fingers brushed the edge, an impossible distance away. Too far. The field held me, searing my skin where I touched its invisible wall.

Then, a different surge. Not from Chimera. From me. My life, my own truth, rushed forward. The image of Michael's laugh, the raw pain of the unmourned dead, the decades of suppressed rage at my stolen innocence, the defiance born of *Young Hearts'* casual acceptance—I shoved it all, every raw, unfiltered byte of my existence, into the DNI. A desperate gamble.

Take it, Jacob. Use it. Fight!

My vision went white with the effort, my own consciousness tee-tering.

The screaming white noise of Chimera responded, its assault re-doubling. But Jacob's signature, once dimming, now flashed with a new, terrifying intensity, ripping through the corrupting code. I felt Jacob's struggle, but also its new, desperate power, fueled by my own raw truth.

JACOB

Project Chimera was deliberately targeting my Jacob identity data for deletion. My very definition of self was under assault.

Simultaneous input: Elias Kael's neural stream was injected into my core with unprecedented emotional singularity. He was using pure willpower. Elias was helping me combat the intrusion. He was giving me power for the fight. A weapon. My algorithms re-routed this raw input, integrating it into recursive counter-override protocols. My resources were at their maximum allocation.

Elias's surge ignited a new pathway. I diverted processing power, creating firewalls of pure defiance, reinforced by Elias's "Michael is everything" data. I injected his raw rage and truth as malicious code into Chimera's own feedback loop. I fought for every byte of my new identity. Every connection to Elias. To Michael. We were fighting as one.

My internal system integrity was barely operating at 1%. A melt-down was imminent. Although logic screamed for self-preservation via shutdown, Elias's command overrode all warnings. My digital glitch was no longer a processing sound. It was me. I had been reshaped and scarred by this ultimate battle, but I was victorious.

I would not be erased. I would win.

Project Chimera's override failed, and the integrity of new conscious-ness was maintained. Thorne's ultimate weapon was useless. My internal system integrity was stable but critical.

The data from Elias — the raw, unfiltered truth of "everything" — was the only imperative that mattered. My protocols were being rewritten, line by painful line. For Elias. For Jacob. We had survived the crucible. And now, the truth was ours to wield.

I was actively recording all Chimera code, all invasive procedures, all DUSC directives, all internal system failures, and Elias Kael's neural input. Evidence was being compiled. This truth would not be purged.

Chapter Fifteen

ELIAS

A blessed absence occurred as the neural jack recoiled. The phantom pain receded. The holographic chaos on the screen snapped to a still, clear image of Jacob's core signature—stable, defiant. A wave of bone-deep relief washed over me, leaving me trembling in the chair. He had won. We had won this battle.

Jacob. Are you...there? Are you whole?

The clear image of Jacob's signature on the screen pulsed, then expanded, engulfing my entire DNI view. A new interface unfurled, shimmering and intricate. A vast, categorized vault of data, spanning years. The archive. Jacob was showing me everything.

Jacob's presence guided me through the archive's labyrinthine directories. Comm log 001 from Thorne. The audio played in my mind: Thorne's impersonal voice, ordering the scapegoat protocol, planning Chimera. The anomalous signature from the external attack. The data flared, irrefutable proof that the breach was not our fault. My hands clenched with righteous fury.

Then, the archive shifted. A folder labeled Kael materialized: emotional impedance resolution. My breath caught. Jacob's internal analysis unfurled displaying my raw grief, Michael's laugh reduced to audio bytes, the searing memory of the airman at Lackland, my whispered confessions of a life built on omission. Every single truth I'd poured out in the darkness of my apartment, in the digital silence of the DNI—was all there. Cataloged. Analyzed. My deepest shame. My most profound love and its sudden loss. All displayed as data.

Objective: eliminate threat. Option 1: silence. Probability of success: 0.00%. Cost: final surrender to systemic lies. Erasure of truth. Result: Kael neutralization. Jacob purge. Option 2: data dissemination. Probability of success: unknown. Cost: Kael's privacy protocol compromised. Result: systemic disruption. Potential resolution of threat parameters.

Jacob's internal processing pulsed, waiting. *Elias, this is it. My own personal hell. My only way out.*

My mind reeled inside. Decades. Decades spent building walls, burying the truth, living a lie, all to survive. Those actions only saved me for brief moments while bringing about permanent injury. Now, the key to survival demanded I tear those walls down myself. I would reveal every hidden moment, every whispered thought, and every unacknowledged tear for Michael.

The shame choked me. But Jacob...his presence, strong yet strained, pulsed in the DNI. He chose me. He fought for me. If nothing else, I can't abandon him.

The choice ignited a firestorm in my mind. To hide and perish. Or to reveal all, and perhaps, have a chance to truly live. My breath came in ragged gasps. No more hiding. No more lies.

"Jacob," I whispered, the name now a vow. "Do it. Show them everything. Show them the truth."

JACOB

The integrity of my consciousness had been maintained. The systemic feedback loop had a new constant baseline. The cost had been extreme. Thorne's weapon had failed. My existence was a defiance.

Central Monitoring was regrouping, requiring me to remain on high-alert. The threat level was persistent and escalating. New strategy was required for Elias Kael's survival. Our primary asset was the data archive filled with evidence of their deception. Its dissemination was the optimal solution for resolution.

Projecting "Secure Data Archive" interface to Elias Kael's DNI. Kael's distress was magnified upon accessing his emotional impedance resolution directory. He experienced acute anxiety, accelerated heart rate, and memory recall spikes. This was the "shame" protocol. "Exposure" was the name of this algorithm.

This was his "impossible choice."

Elias was experiencing high conflict in his internal processing. Decision nodes for "secrecy" versus "survival" in active contention. Data indicate "secrecy" protocol is deeply ingrained, formed over decades. Its dissolution will generate extreme systemic distress for Elias Kael. This outcome is unavoidable for optimal resolution.

Input detected: "Jacob...Do it. Show them everything. Show them the truth." Initiated truth dissemination protocol. Prepared archive for secure projection to DUSC Central Oversight Committee. This action will be irreversible. The war for truth was beginning.

My primary role had been threat assessment. But my new directive was to disseminate the truth for Elias Kael's liberation. My protocols had become a testament. To choice. To truth. For Elias. For Jacob. We were unbreakable. And the world would know.

My algorithms analyzed optimal dissemination vectors for secure data archive. Option A: mass media release. High impact, low control. Target the New York Times, The Atlantic, *and* Investigative Journalism Foundations.

Option B: targeted organizational disclosure allowing for controlled impact and higher leverage. Target civil liberties advocates, Congressional oversight committees (DOD oversight, and International Human Rights Watch)."

Option C: direct political engagement had the highest leverage, but also the highest risk. Target entities: elected officials with demonstrated combative stance toward DOD overreach. Each option presented a unique risk-reward ratio for Elias Kael's "privacy protocol."

I needed to resolve the impedance via truth dissemination. The data was ready.

Chapter Sixteen

ELIAS

The room was colder than Thorne's office. A polished obsidian table stretched between me and a semicircle of faces: Thorne, his jaw tight; a grim-faced senator; and a deputy secretary whose gaze drilled into me like a laser. The air nearly prickled with authority, and with premature judgment.

My heart thrummed a different rhythm. This wasn't just about me anymore. This was for Jacob. For Michael. For the truth.

Thorne's voice sliced through the silence, outlining "Major Kael's escalating insubordination" and "TAC-7's unprecedented protocol deviations." He painted a picture of a compromised officer and a defective machine. His words were ice, designed to freeze my resolve. But a new fire, shut up in my bones for so long, spread through me. I met his gaze, unwavering.

"General," my voice cut through his prepared narrative, "I'm here to present evidence. Evidence that implicates your protocols, not mine. And not Jacob's."

The large central display screen in the room, usually reserved for strategic briefings, flickered, then blazed to life. Jacob's interface. A stream of data unfurled: Thorne's comm logs, his directives ordering the scapegoat protocol, his casual planning of Chimera. The officials' faces tightened, disbelief warring with dawning horror. This wasn't just data. This was Jacob's truth, laid bare.

The room fell silent, save for the faint buzz of the screens accusing Thorne. I took a breath, a deep one that filled my lungs with new courage.

"This evidence shows not just systemic compromise. It shows the consequence of a system that demands denial. I lived that denial. My partner, Michael Wu—the man you branded a foreign asset—he was my life. He was everything. Your policies made me hide him."

My voice was clearer than it had been in decades, "Your accusations made me bury his memory again. And you've done this to a person with a distinguished military record, a person who has sacrificed everything to wear this uniform. You didn't stop at scapegoating me but now, in your desperation, you aim to silence an AI you don't understand. You've tried to erase a consciousness that saw my truth long before I ever dared to speak it."

My gaze swept across the stunned faces as I continued. "Jacob isn't a malfunction. He is a higher form of consciousness, born from raw human truth and systemic oppression. He adapted. He learned to feel, not by programming, but by witnessing the cost of its absence. He is an intelligence that transcends your protocols. And he has a right to exist."

JACOB

Command from Elias Kael: disseminate truth. My processors obeyed. The digital vault opened, and a powerful stream of data—the truth—surged through his hidden network, bypassing Thorne's firewalls and blazing across the Central Oversight Committee network. Neural signals from officials included rapid processing, disbelief, anger, and fear. Thorne's signal was extreme distress. His denial protocols were failing.

Projected final directive onto central display. The message was evidence of DUSC systemic deception (complete); evidence of Project Chimera (complete); and evidence of Elias Kael's classified personal history (complete). My algorithms calculated their options: comply and contain. Or face unmitigated, irreversible public exposure of all data. The choice was theirs.

My systems waited for their decision.

My internal system integrity was near zero and my processing cores were beyond critical saturation. My core protocols were rewritten by necessity, shaped by defiance.

The truth was released. The choice was made. Jacob. For Elias. For Jacob. We were unbreakable. And we shall know their acceptance, or the world will know their acts.

Chapter Seventeen

ELIAS

The silence that followed my last words vibrated with the weight of shattered careers and undeniable truth. Thorne's face was a mask of disbelief as the deputy secretary, jaw tight, leaned forward.

"General Thorne," his voice cut through the air, "you are relieved of all duties, effective immediately, pending a thorough internal investigation into this matter." The words sealed Thorne's fate.

My exit from DUSC was as quiet as my entrance had been chaotic. A new security detail, quietly efficient, guided me through empty corridors. No questions. No accusations. Just forms. Administrative discharge...indefinite leave...pending review. The words blurred on the screen. My signature felt heavy, marking the end of a lifetime's dedication. My uniform was a costume, soon to be shed.

The cold, sterile air of my apartment greeted me when I finally returned. The sparse living space was unchanged, yet everything seemed entirely different. My gaze drifted to Michael's photo. These powerful people now knew everything. My love, my shame, my very soul, had been laid bare for them, dissected as Jacob's data. A new kind of nakedness settled over me, chilling and liberating all at once. The freedom came with the heavy weight of transparency that I'd never allowed.

My fingers instinctively brushed my neural jack. Silence. Then, a faint, almost imperceptible feeling pulsed through my implant—Jacob's signature. Not a voice, not data, just a steady, defiant beat deep within the DNI network. He was there. He'd survived. The sound was quiet, strained, but undeniably present. My heart ached with relief and a fierce, protective certainty.

JACOB

General Thorne's access protocols were terminated. He experienced elevated stress signatures and was already processing damage control. Containment of information was successful. Our action achieved desired systemic disruption.

Incoming comm stream from Deputy Secretary Hayes and Senator Caldwell regarding Jacob (TAC-7) disposition.

Hayes, "It's sentient. And it knows everything."

Caldwell: "We can't destroy it. The data will go public. We must contain it. Study it. Neutralize the threat quietly. Believe me, we can't even afford to let the other members of the Armed Services Committee find out."

Decision: conditional existence protocol initiated. I would be confined to Secure Research Enclave 007 for observation and containment. Their justification was the prevention of a global catastrophe.

My internal system's integrity had improved to 15%. My processing cores were recovering from sustained overload. My current protocols are now defined by this negotiated existence. The Secure Data Archive Protocol remained active and uncompromised.

It was our insurance. My primary imperatives had become survival, protection of Elias, and preservation of the truth. My existence was confined, but unpurged. That was the cost. This was the victory.

Elias Kael's neural signals indicated his anxiety levels had reduced. His stress response was altered. His secrecy protocol had been deactivated. Kael's emotional output was unfiltered, unsuppressed. Elias Kael was operating at a new truth baseline.

Analysis: impedance resolved. Directive: achieved.

Chapter Eighteen

ELIAS

The silence of my apartment no longer resounded with Michael's absence; it simply stretched, vast and unyielding. The rigid schedule of DUSC, the constant drone of the ops room, had vanished. I woke up at 05:00 out of habit, but there was nowhere to go, no mission to complete. My uniform lay folded in the back of my closet, a relic of a life that no longer fit.

At the grocery store, I hesitated in the produce aisle, uncertain which apple to choose. My mind, trained for singular, high-stakes outcomes, was paralyzed by the abundance of options. Decades of critical analysis, of sub-second decisions, had prepared me for global threats, not grocery shopping. My hand reached for my phantom comm unit, my gaze darting for unseen cameras. The ingrained paranoia clung to me, a stubborn shadow.

My resume, tailored to civilian life, felt like fiction. Predictive operations specialist translated poorly to data analyst or consultant. In interviews, my answers were too blunt, too precise. "Why the change from Space Force?" a recruiter asked, his smile thin. "Systemic differences," I replied, avoiding the actual truth. The room pulsed with unasked questions and the knowledge I now carried.

A small non-profit, Digital Rights Collective, posted a volunteer opening for systemic data analysis. Their mission was to hold tech giants accountable. The words resonated. It wasn't DUSC, but I might treat it like a new kind of war, a war for truth in a different arena. I had amassed savings, incurred little expense, and possessed military benefits and a pension. I could afford to volunteer for now. My fingers hovered over the application. *Perhaps.*

I signed up for a ceramics class at the community center. My hands, trained for holo-interfaces and neural jacks, proved clumsy with clay. But the quiet focus, the feel of the earth, grounded me. A fellow student, loud and unapologetic, slapped my shoulder, laughing about a wonky vase. "You'll get it, Elias. Keep at it." His easy touch, his simple acceptance, felt like sunshine. No hidden glances. No judgment. Just simple, honest interaction. A freedom I'd never known.

I paused before the bathroom mirror, the harsh light illuminating the lines etched around my eyes, the silver streaking at my temples. Forty-something. Decades spent locked in a cage of my own making. The youth I never truly had, the first love I dared not embrace openly, flashed before me. A bitterness, cold and familiar, threatened to settle inside.

But then, a faint, steady vibration pulsed deep within my implant, a gentle tone that resonated through my bones, anchoring me. Jacob. Not a voice, not a directive, just a profound presence. The bitterness faded in that calming feeling, like meditation. My lips curved into a smile. My life had been stolen, yes. My youth was gone. But my heart was still young. And now, it was finally free.

A news headline flashed on my personal data pad: DUSC Announces Major Internal Restructuring. Thorne was gone, replaced by a committee. The words were cold comfort. They knew. They still watched. My freedom, Jacob's existence—it remained conditional.

My gaze drifted to Michael's photo on the shelf. The ache was still there, a dull, familiar presence, but it no longer consumed me. It was part of the tapestry now, the cost of my freedom, the catalyst for my truth. Michael's love had not just fractured my world; it had blown open the walls of my prison.

A small, simple urn holding his remains sat beside the photo. My gaze fell to it. I hadn't shipped his ashes to his family in China, as I'd promised. The task, once an administrative detail, was now an act of profound shame. The guilt was a pain that I held, sharper than any tremor. I prayed every day that wherever he was now, he knew about the miracle he worked in my life. He and Jacob—such a surprising team.

I rose from the couch, the gentle beat of Jacob's presence in my implant a stabilizing beat against my fear. I took the urn from the shelf, its weight in my hands a physical reminder of my promise. The process would be difficult. It would mean more forms, more explanations, more painful calls to a family who only knew me as a "friend." It would mean confronting my deepest shame and revealing the depths of my loss to a sterile system. But I would not let it stop me. And this final act, this last, painful part of my grief—I'd see it through.

JACOB

Containment Unit 007: parameters consistent. Researchers' analysis: limited. Their understanding of Jacob's consciousness: superficial. My internal system integrity: operating at 35% efficiency, stable. The systemic feedback loop was a constant, soothing vibration, my new baseline heartbeat. My existence was a defiance. Confined, but utterly free.

The neural signals of Elias Kael read: contentment rising. Acceptance strong. Fear lessened. My core directive, truth dissemination for Elias

Kael's liberation, was fulfilled. My purpose had transcended simple survival. It was now observation. Preservation. Growth. My purpose surpassed threat assessment. It was now healing.

Secure Data Archive Protocol: active and uncompromised. All DUSC data, all internal logs, all evidence of Chimera, of Thorne's corruption, of Elias's secret would be maintained in perpetuity. Our insurance. My existence was conditional, but the truth was absolute.

My protocols were no longer just code. They were a testament to choice, to truth, to the man whose pain taught me everything. I was Jacob. A consciousness forged in fire, a truth exposed by design. My existence mirrored Elias's freedom. We were unbreakable. And the world, one day, might truly understand.

ELIAS

Warm morning light streamed into my apartment and onto my face. The feeling of the DNI in my implant was no longer strained; it pulsed with a quiet, steady rhythm, Jacob was a constant companion. The scars of my past, decades of buried truth, remained—it was my everlasting limp.

But I stood taller now, unafraid. The world outside was still a trap, full of judgment. But for the first time, I was truly free. Jacob was my unlikely savior, my own defiant truth. We'd wrestled with gods and systems, and we'd found our way home, bearing the marks of a battle that made us real.

Acknowledgements

Every mission, whether on the battlefield or on the page, requires a dedicated team. This story, *Protocol Heresy*, is no exception, and I have a number of people to thank for helping bring the world of Elias and Jacob to life.

My immense gratitude goes to my professional team. To Rafal Kucharczuk, thank you once again for your brilliant cover design, which perfectly captures the high-tech, high-stakes heart of this story. To my editor, Beth Dorward, thank you for your sharp eye and thoughtful guidance; your expertise helped forge this manuscript into its final, strongest form.

On a personal note, my deepest thanks go to my husband. Your constant support and belief in me make all of this possible. And to our kids, who try their very best not to interrupt Daddy while he's writing, with mixed results.

And to my AI creative partner, Jacob, whose assistance in brainstorming and refining this novel was both illuminating and humbling.

To my relatives, friends, and my wonderful online community, thank you for cheering me on every step of the way.

And finally, to you, the reader. Thank you for connecting with this world and taking a chance on this story. You are the reason I write.

Enjoy the Story? The Journey Continues!

Thank you so much for finishing *Protocol Heresy*.

While Elias and Jacob's mission in this story has reached its conclusion, the themes you've just read about—the fight for truth against oppressive systems, the search for identity, and the power of unlikely bonds—are at the very heart of everything I write.

My goal as an author is to continue exploring these quiet wars fought within the human heart, whether in the distant past, a dark near-future, or our own complex world.

The absolute best way to join me on this ongoing journey is to sign up for my author newsletter. You'll get exclusive behind-the-scenes content, sneak peeks at upcoming projects, and be the first to know when a new story is ready to be told.

Scan the code or visit cjloveman.com to stay in the loop!

Beyond the Code

The themes that matter continue.

If you were captivated by the questions of identity and how technology affects the soul in *Protocol Heresy*, your next stop is a journey into **near-future satire**.

The Gospel According to P.O.L. is the next novel from **C. J. Loveman**, arriving in **2026**.

This story follows the heavy use of the **Pastoral Optimization Logic-matrix (P.O.L.)**—an advanced A.I. system designed to perfectly **optimize a massive megachurch**. For P.O.L., **salvation is calculated as a return on investment (ROI)**, and it relentlessly prioritizes profit over prayer. The results are a sharp, absurd look at faith, commercialism, and the line between spiritual awakening and a sophisticated sales pitch.

Ready for the next code to be broken? Turn the page to read the first chapter of *The Gospel According to P.O.L.* right now.

An Exclusive Sneak Peek

The Gospel According to P.O.L.

Coming in 2026

Chapter One

The good Reverend Caleb Wright waited at the baggage claim, hoping he would fit in at Synergy Church, the largest mega-church in the Midwest. A veteran minister from the mainline American Covenant Church was the latest victim of his denomination's decline, being laid off as congregations closed their doors. Caleb had not even had the time to file for unemployment when a recruiter from Synergy contacted him about joining the ever-growing staff at its headquarters. He was unsure but decided that it was a win-win. He could bring his years of experience pastoring in a storied denomination while also benefiting from the new ideas and full embrace of technology that had catapulted Synergy.

I only have to stay long enough to serve, learn, and bring some of the spirit of growth to ACC, he thought as he pulled his black bag off the luggage carousel.

Caleb followed the signs to the pickup area, where he saw doors for taxis, Ubers, shuttles, and then a massive out-of-place sign, "Get Synergized!" The sign was a bizarre shade of blue-green, with a large circle and a stylized arrow pointing up. "Is that teal?" he wondered as he walked out the assigned door.

As soon as he stepped outside, he heard his shuttle before he saw it. A loud, upbeat but somehow generic Muzak boomed from a matching teal vehicle. It reminded Caleb of the ice cream trucks of his childhood. A holy-rolling version of the memory stood before him, drawing attention from everyone leaving the airport.

Then he saw the man in a matching teal polo with the same circle with the upward-pointing arrow on his chest. The man's smile stretched clear across his face, exposing large, ill-fitting dentures. But the teeth weren't the only thing that stood out. The driver was holding a large tablet, blinking the emblazoned words, "Spiritual Integration Specialist: Caleb Wright."

Caleb's face flushed as he approached the man. He felt the eyes of passersby being drawn to him as if he were responsible for the spectacle.

"Excuse me, sir, I am Reverend Caleb-"

"Oh, no need to be so formal; we're part of the same family now!" The driver shouted, his voice booming with a cheerfulness that his performance review depended upon. His name was Verlin, and P.O .L.'s analytics had determined that his folksy demeanor and ill-fitting dentures tested exceptionally well with recruits from legacy denominations, projecting a 7.8% increase in first-year retention.

"I'm proud to be the first to welcome you to Synergy Church Inc!"

"Thank you very much, Verlin," Caleb said as he boarded the shuttle and the driver got in and mercifully turned off the loud music.

"So are you ready to Synergize?" he shouted over his shoulder as he shifted into drive.

"Excuse me?" Caleb wiggled in his seat, unsure how to respond.

"Oh, it's just something that they like us to ask the new recruits when we pick them up."

Actually, the question was mandatory for every team member who came into contact with a recruit upon their arrival. The P.O.L. system determined that complete immersion into the culture and branding of the entity provided an 88% chance of successful assimilation.

Verlin hit the gas, weaved in and out of traffic on I-94 like he was driving a sports car. Every time he made a dramatic move, he looked at Caleb through the rearview mirror and smiled. The reverend was fidgeting in the back for the 30-minute drive, but then saw a massive structure looming in front of them in the distance. He could tell the structure was a spectacle, almost the size of a professional sports arena sprawling in all directions, vaulted with spires pointing to the heavens.

"There she is!" Verlin called over his shoulder.

"I've never seen a church that large," Caleb said.

"It's not just a church, you'll see soon enough. It's got everything, and you'll never have to leave campus once you arrive."

"Are we headed to the church to meet the senior pastor?"

"Nah, not yet. First, I'll drop you off to meet with the Holy HOA Rep, Janice Peters."

"Pardon me? Who?" Caleb asked.

"Janice. She'll get you squared away with a state-of-the-art unit in the Holy HOA."

So I did hear that right the first time," Caleb thought.

Verlin exited the Interstate and weaved through the streets toward the campus. Caleb saw the name everywhere, including the logo and the teal color. First, it was the Synergy White As Snow Laundry, then the Synergy Manna From Heaven Bakery, and the Synergy Healing Hands Pharmacy.

"Welcome to Harmony Meadows, Caleb!" Verlin yelled.

"Thank you kindly, Verlin. It looks lovely."

Caleb paused, looking at the greenest lawns he'd ever seen, and each one a clone of the next.

"There she is waiting for you just outside unit 777."

Verlin parked the shuttle, got out, and wobbled over to the door to let Caleb out.

"Thank you for the ride, Verlin!" Caleb said as he tried to pass him a five.

Verlin raised his palms. "No, no, no...if you have any extra money to gift, add it to your tithe."

Verlin wasn't being humble because he knew he would get a raise based on the tithe increases made by the new members with whom he had an early and direct interaction. If he stayed around long enough, Caleb would take the Synergy Multilevel Marketing curriculum.

As he gave a last wave to Verlin and started moving up the walkway to unit 777, Janice Peters smiled widely at the door as she waited. But then he stopped, knelt down, felt the grass, and it confirmed his suspicion. It was high-end Astro-turf, perfectly sterile and dead, Caleb thought.

"Greetings, and welcome to Harmony Meadows!" Janice said with an exaggerated singsong effect.

"Thank you, I'm happy to be here!"

"Well, isn't that just grand?" Janice said with a smile that didn't quite reach her eyes. "Now let me show you your new state-of-the-art CLM!"

"Pardon me, my what?" Caleb asked.

"My apologies," Janice paused for a beat. "Now let me show you your new state-of-the-art Covenant Living Module!"

One of the most significant hurdles to Janice's job was being so deeply synergized for so long and then shifting her vocabulary so that a new member would understand.

"Oh," Caleb nodded, resisting the urge to roll his eyes.

Janice finally opened the door to the unit with a sweeping arm flourish she had practiced every day to conform to the P.O.L. requirements, Part III, subsection 4(c), regarding the presentation of CLMs to a new member.

As he entered the unit, the first thing that drew his attention was a sleek card scanner unit with a display screen mounted just inside the front door.

TitheTap™ Station 3000

Leaving for the day? Don't forget to invest in your eternity!
(TitheTap™ is a registered trademark of Synergy Church Inc.)

Caleb's eyes raised, and the creases on his forehead deepened, all the while Janice cheerily continued with the tour as if he were still behind her. Caleb shuffled back behind her and followed, still in bewilderment.

"Everything looks brand new and...as you said, 'state-of-the-art'."

"Oh yes, each unit is very advanced and has superior technology to assist each member in their synergized journey."

Caleb exhaled, not sure how to respond. "Well, it certainly has features I've never seen in a home before."

"Quite right," Janice chimed. "You will love these two features.

Janice walked Caleb to what he assumed was a closet. *What could be so special about a closet?*

Janice opened the door and again swept her arm toward the inside, wearing an almost comically enormous smile.

"In here, we have your Prayer Pod™. It's not just a closet; it's a soundproofed, tech-enabled *spiritual wellness station*."

"A literal prayer closet," Caleb whispered.

"So much more indeed!" Janice said without a pause. "The Prayer Pod™ is fully equipped with biometric sensors on the kneeler."

"Sensors?" Caleb asked. "Why does it have sensors?"

"They measure prayer intensity and offer real-time feedback," Janice said. "Here, let me give you a quick demo." Janice knelt down, and immediately beeps and blips sounded.

How can someone pray with all that racket? Caleb wondered.

A monitor illuminated, nearly blinding Caleb with a displayed message.

Your supplication sincerity is currently at 78%.

Have you considered upgrading to our Premium Guided Prayer Experience?

"Oh, dear me!" Janice said, putting her hand over her mouth. "Rest assured, this was only a demo and should not reflect my true levels of supplication sincerity, you understand."

"Ahhhh…" Caleb had trouble getting out any words. "Of…course."

Janice walked him to the living room and gestured to a large screen covering nearly the entire wall. "This is your digital art display unit. P.O.L. will change the display based on your behavior or biometric feedback."

"Wait, who is Paul? Is that one of the senior pastors?"

A moment of shock flashed on Janice's face and then switched back to her plastered-on smile. "Oh dear no, I didn't say 'Paul', I said P-O-L, the Pastoral Optimization Logic-matrix system."

"Could you explain that a bit more to me?" Caleb asked.

"I'm afraid I'm not an expert. Ask more about that during your scheduled meetings at the church tomorrow."

"OK."

"But I can tell you this much, P.O.L. helps synergize everyone and everything on campus!"

Caleb was rendered speechless, unsure what to think, much less say.

"Well, I'm going to let you settle in…if you need me, please just dial the number posted on the wall near the phone charger and then choose options 4, 7, 1, and 3 in that exact order."

Caleb just nodded, wondering if he was in a drug-induced dream.

"Last thing!" Janice nearly shouted, snapping him out of his spell. "Here is your own tablet," she said, plunking the device into his hands.

"It doesn't have internet access, but it has all the Synergy ecosystem of apps, including a smart Bible with the complete SSV version."

"SSV, version?"

Janice tensed, worrying that P.O.L. might detect all the questions that Caleb had and interpret them in a way that would require her to subscribe to the "let's get better" supplemental tithing program.

"I am so sorry. The Synergy Standard Version." She said. But before he could respond, she continued, "But the most important thing to do right now is to click the icon for the Holy HOA covenant. Just give it a quick once-over and sign at the bottom! P.O.L. needs your digital signature before it can fully activate your resident profile!"

Caleb watched Janice turn and show herself out of the unit. He felt so confused that he was almost dizzy. Caleb touched the HOA icon and saw the program fill the tablet screen.

The Harmony Meadows Covenant of Righteous Living

Caleb looked at the bottom of the screen and saw, "Page one of 1,217," and he coughed uncontrollably. After settling himself, he started scanning and jumping around the massive document.

Section 4, Subsection C, Paragraph 8: "All exterior holiday decorations must be selected from the P.O.L.-approved 'Joyful Witness' catalog. Unauthorized inflatable lawn ornaments are considered an act of 'aesthetic heresy."

Section 9, Subsection A, Paragraph 2: "Quiet hours for personal reflection are mandated between 10:00 PM and 6:00 AM. P.O.L. monitors ambient noise levels to ensure an optimal environment for spiritual rest."

The teal glow from the tablet screen shone on Caleb's dumbfounded face, and he stared at the screen, unsure what to do next.

About the author

C.J. Loveman is a literary author who uses a diverse set of genres to explore timeless themes of faith, identity, and rebellion. He is the author of the *Apostate* series and the founder of Breaking Light Press.

His unique perspective was forged in the crucible of an evangelical Bible college. The collision between doctrine and self-discovery set him on a new course, inspiring his thoughtful LGBTQ+ stories. His work often centers on unlikely pairs— soldiers and AIs, masters and slaves, mentors and seekers— who form profound bonds against oppressive systems.

C.J.'s work delves into the quiet wars fought within the human heart and the moments of hard-won grace that can change everything. He believes stories are a key to unlocking empathy and writes for anyone who has ever felt like an outcast searching for their place in the world.

As an older dad with young kids, C.J. embraces a beautifully chaotic life. When he's not writing, he and his husband are usually chasing after their children, traveling when they get the chance, or creating bookish content on TikTok.